SOOTY

STORY BOOK

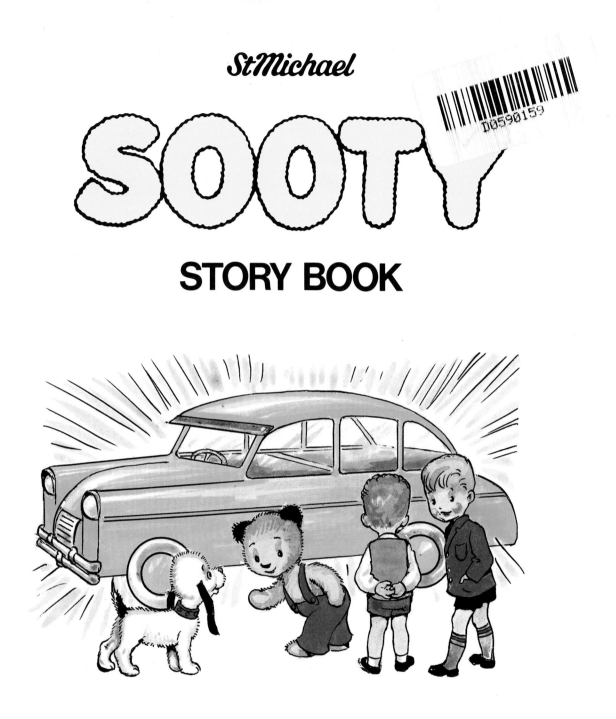

Sooty Lives Up To His Name

One day, Matthew decided to have his chimney swept. Sweep told Sooty, and said that he'd like to watch the chimney sweep very much. But Sooty had a better idea than that.

'Let's sweep the chimney ourselves whilst Matthew is out,' he said. 'It will be a lovely surprise for him!'

Sweep went outside to keep a look out for Matthew. Sooty found a brush, climbed into the fireplace and peered up the chimney. It was terribly dark. He didn't like the look of it very much, but he kept thinking how surprised Matthew would be when he came home and found it clean.

So he started to climb the chimney, brushing all the soot off as he went. When he finally got to the top, he felt rather pleased with himself and started to wave at Sweep down below. Then he suddenly disappeared down the chimney. Sweep heard Sooty coming down the chimney, but when he got to the sitting room, all he could see was a great big heap of soot on the carpet. What a surprise Sweep got when he saw the heap move and two eyes look out!

'Is that you, Sooty?' asked Sweep nervously.

Sooty shook the soot away from his mouth and nodded.

'I fell down the chimney,' he explained.

Sweep took one look at the carpet and then ran into the hall, just to make sure that Matthew hadn't come back! It was lucky Sweep did, because the first thing he saw when he got there was a vacuum cleaner.

Sooty was pleased when Sweep pushed the vacuum cleaner into the room. He really had made a terrible mess! He put the plug in and switched it on as fast as he could.

It didn't take all that long to suck up all the soot, and by the time they had swept the carpet and dusted the furniture, it looked quite tidy.

Sooty was very dirty too, so Sweep turned the vacuum cleaner onto him and tried to clean him up. Of course, Matthew was very surprised to find them with the vacuum cleaner when he came back a few minutes later. When he saw Sooty's black face he began to look very puzzled indeed.

'What have you been up to, Sooty?' he asked sternly.

Sooty climbed up and whispered in his ear.

'Sweeping my chimney?' said Matthew in amazement. 'But what's happened to all the soot?'

Sooty and Sweep looked very pleased. Sooty climbed up and put a very black paw on Matthew's ear. 'It's magic,' he said proudly. 'We've conjured it away!'

Matthew looked doubtfully at Sooty, and then at the chimney. He couldn't see any soot, so perhaps it *was* magic.

Sooty nearly offered to do something else tricky, like mending the roof or dusting the china.

'Don't you dare,' whispered Sweep just in time. 'And *don't* offer to do the vacuuming either, because the vacuum's full up with soot!'

Sooty thought for a moment, and then agreed that perhaps he had done enough good deeds for one day.

Matthew had saved quite a lot of money by not calling in the proper chimney sweep. So he gave Sooty and Sweep some extra pocket money.

'I think that you ought to buy some soap,' he said, 'so that Sooty can finish cleaning his sooty face!'

Sooty *and* Sweep had certainly lived up to their names, anyway. But I do hope that they aren't around when Matthew empties his vacuum cleaner, don't you?

Sooty's Washing Day

One day, Sooty had a very good idea for making pocket money. He advertised "Sooty's Washing Service" and promised to do bundles of washing for his neighbours, at a small charge.

Unfortunately, the washing machine wasn't used to doing so much work and it soon broke down. Sooty had to do a mountain of washing the old-fashioned way, with a washboard and a big tub.

He soon realized just what a good invention washing machines are! It took him ages to scrub the clothes clean, and he wished he'd never advertised at all.

The problem didn't end there, because all the clothes and sheets had to be dried. And everyone was coming back to collect their bundles at five o'clock! Poor old Sooty; he hung everything out on the line, but there was no breeze at all that day.

Sooty tried everything. He tried flapping a towel to make a breeze. Sweep even tried blowing the washing himself, but he couldn't keep it up for long.

Sooty got very worried.

'This is an emergency,' he said. 'I think I'll have to make use of my magic wand.'

He stood in front of the washing line, waved his wand and said:

'Izzy-whizzy, land and sea,
Bring a wind to dry for me!'

As soon as he had finished, the wind started. It became so strong that Sooty and Sweep had to grab hold of the washing line post to stop themselves being blown away!

They couldn't save the clothes. Every last piece of washing sailed off: socks, towels, sheets, trousers and hankies. Sooty's magic had been a bit too strong!

'Well, we'll just have to catch it all,' said Sooty. He jumped into his little car and raced off up the road, following the washing. But the wind didn't stop, and the washing was carried right over the houses. Sooty waved his wand and shouted, but it was no use.

The trouble was, all the people living in the houses along the way saw the flying washing too.

'I must be dreaming. I thought I saw my shirt up in the sky!' said one.

'What's going on?' shouted a policeman. 'Aren't they my socks flying away? I was just going to collect them!'

They were all very annoyed with Sooty.

'You won't get any money until you've returned our washing,' they cried. 'In fact, you'll have to pay us for all the clothes you've lost!'

Sooty knew that they were quite right. So he closed his
eyes and thought of a really strong spell to stop the wind.
Then he shouted at the top of his voice:

'You've done your work, now that's enough,
Stop and drop the washing stuff!'

At once the wind died down and the washing fell to the
ground.

'Well,' said Sweep. 'Next time, I think you should do
your washing and drying the old-fashioned way.'

'But I did,' said Sooty puzzled.

'I mean without a magic wand!' chuckled Sweep.

Sooty Removals Limited

One day, Sooty and Sweep saw an advertisement in the local papershop. It said:

"Willing workers needed. Come to 13 Cherry Cross Road at 2.30 p.m. Bring your own aprons."

'That sounds like cookery!' said Sooty. 'Let's do it. We might get some cake as well as some pocket money!' But when the two friends turned up at Cherry Cross Road with their aprons on, all they could see was a large van parked outside number 13. The house itself looked rather empty.

'Oh dear,' said Sweep. 'It doesn't look like a cookery job at all. It looks much more like a removal job.'

Sweep was right. A large grumpy man came out of the house along with a rather thin rude one.

'If you want some pocket money you'd better get started on this lot,' said the fat man, pointing at the van. It was full of heavy furniture.

'We're going for a tea-break! Make sure you've finished by the time we get back.' And with that the two men disappeared off up the road.

Sooty and Sweep got started. At first they were very keen but they soon found that a lot of the furniture was just too heavy! They picked up the sofa, and although Sweep

got the front end out all right, Sooty found that he was stuck at the other end. He couldn't jump off the back of the van without dropping the sofa!

'Perhaps this job wasn't such a good idea, after all,' said Sooty. Sweep definitely agreed with that! He seemed to get left with all the weight whenever Sooty got stuck or dropped things. Eventually they managed to move some of the furniture out into the road, but it was no good leaving it there!

'Let's have a rest,' said Sooty. Sweep flopped down with relief. He really was exhausted!

Just then the two grumpy men came back from their tea-break.

'So you're resting on the job, are you?' said the fat one. 'Well, that isn't good enough at all. You certainly won't be getting a tea-break today! Look, you haven't even unloaded all the furniture yet! You are lazy!'

Sooty didn't know what to say, he was so cross. And Sweep couldn't say anything either, because he was so out of breath!

But Sooty always comes up with a good idea in a crisis; it doesn't always work but he always tries something!

He got his magic wand out and thought very hard indeed. Then he said these words:

> 'Izzy, whizzy, fly into the air,
> And sort yourself out over there!'

For once, Sooty's magic worked, and all the furniture flew up into the air. Sooty was a little worried where it would land, but it all floated through the door as easy as winking.

The grumpy men were so astonished that they jumped into their van and drove off at top speed! The owners of the house looked out of the window to see what all the fuss was about and saw exactly what was happening.

The owners were delighted that Sooty had done the work so quickly, and they gave him quite a bit of pocket money.

They even made a sign to put up against the clock, which had floated straight to the right place.

The grumpy removers were never seen again. In fact, they probably gave up removing altogether, when they saw what sort of competition they were up against!

Perhaps they learnt a lesson and stopped being grumpy, too. This was one occasion when Sooty's magic did a lot of good for everyone.

'I only wish your magic worked as well every time,' said Sweep. And Sooty secretly thought that, too!

Gone Fishing

Sooty was being very mysterious, very mysterious indeed. He had been up in his bedroom for absolutely ages, and Sweep just couldn't wait any longer to find out what Sooty was doing!

Sweep knocked on his door.

'Sooty, are you in there?' he asked, knowing full well that Sooty *was* in there!

'Come in,' said Sooty. Sweep didn't need to be asked twice!

A moment or two later, Sooty was showing Sweep a huge pile of money.

'There,' he said proudly. 'I've saved up enough money to buy the best fishing rod anyone could possibly want. We can go and buy one today and go fishing at the seaside as soon as the weather is right. Won't that be fun!'

Sweep wasn't so sure.

'Do you know all about fishing then?' he asked. 'Well, no, but I'm sure it's easy,' said Sooty confidently. 'Don't worry, it will be great fun. We can catch a fish for Matthew's tea. He will be surprised!'

Sooty went out and bought a fishing rod, as well as some hooks and lines, a basket to put the fish in, and a stool to sit on. Most importantly of all he made a big picnic and took some extra bread as bait.

As they walked to the station,
the people in the street waved goodbye.

Sooty smiled and waved back. Sweep looked worried.

When they got to the seaside, Sooty found a good place
to sit on the pier, where there were lots of fishermen
catching quite big fish.

'You wait and see,' said Sooty. 'I'll catch much bigger
ones than those!'

Sooty was right . . .

At first it was rather boring and nothing happened.
Sweep yawned and was just about to fall asleep when . . .

'Look out!' shouted one of the fishermen.

A huge fish had swallowed Sooty's bait! It gave one big
tug, and pulled Sooty right off the pier and into the water.

23

'Oh no!' cried Sweep. 'Someone help him. He'll drown!'

Sweep couldn't understand why everyone on the pier was cheering. He almost jumped in to save poor Sooty himself; but he couldn't swim either.

Then Sweep realized what was happening. Sooty was being pulled along by the fish like a waterskier! The fish turned and swam to the shore. It swam so fast that it was soon high and dry on the sand, along with poor old Sooty.

'Splendid catch!' said an important-looking gentleman who had run up to Sooty. 'You've won the fishing competition! I'm the Mayor, and I hereby present you with the prize for catching this fish!'

'I think the fish caught me!' said Sooty chuckling to himself.

Sooty and the Cleaning Spell

It was a beautiful, sunny day.

'Let's relax, put away the spells book, make a picnic and go into the garden,' said Sooty.

Sweep thought that was a great idea, and he started to make the sandwiches straight away. He had just finished putting apricot jam on some bread when there was a knock at the door. Sooty opened it to find two very glum-looking little boys. They were Matthew's cousins, who had come to stay for the summer holidays.

'Hello,' said Sooty. 'You're just in time to come on a picnic.'

'We can't come,' they said. 'We were playing football near the neighbour's car and we've accidentally splashed it with mud.'

'Hmm, I see,' said Sooty.
'It looks as if I'm going to have to use my
magic after all. But it will be worth it. I'll get the
car clean in a jiffy, then we'll all be able to go on a picnic.'
With that, he strode confidently out of the door, his book
under his arm.

'Right,' said Sooty, when he got to the garage door, 'I'll just look up the car-cleaning spell in my book. Ah, here we are,' he said as he found the right page. Then he stood in front of the car, pointed his magic wand at it and said:

'Soapy flakes and bubbles too,
Give this car a good shampoo!'

As soon as Sooty said "shampoo" the car started to bubble like a washtub, and in next to no time it was completely covered in soapy bubbles.

Everyone was pleased! All they had to do now was wipe the bubbles off the car and it would be clean and sparkling . . .

But unfortunately, someone had left a packet of soapflakes on the back seat. As soon as the magic reached the packet, all the soapflakes began to bubble up, and before you could say "soapsud" the car was full of them!

It quite frightened Sooty when he saw all the bubbles floating out of the car, and it wasn't long before the air was so thick with them that he couldn't see Sweep at all! He could *hear* his friends all right because they were all shouting at him to stop the magic.

Sooty liked bubbles in the bath, but this *was* a bit much. He would have stopped the magic, but before he could think of a proper spell something terrible happened. The car rose up from the ground and floated out of the garage!

Sooty was very upset. He seemed to have made everything much worse with his spell. But what upset him most of all was that the car floated over the garden fishpond and stayed there, ready to splash into the water at any time!

Fortunately, it gave Sooty a very good idea.

'I know, we'll hose it down,' he said, and ran off to fetch the hose-pipe.

"WHOOOOSH!" went the water. It hit the car so hard that it shot right across to the other side of the pond and then onto the pathway. It was very lucky that it did, because the water burst all the bubbles and the car dropped to the ground.

Sooty felt rather pleased with himself, although the car fell with a bit of a thud, which can't have done it much good at all. In fact, it made such a loud bang that the man who owned it came out of the house to see what was going on.

The two boys explained that they had been cleaning his car. Sooty felt rather annoyed when they said this, because, after all, they hadn't really cleaned it at all. Sooty's magic had done that!

It didn't really matter *who* had done it. All that mattered was that the neighbour was very pleased indeed with his shiny car. He just couldn't understand how it had got to the other side of the garden! In return, he gave them all some pocket money so that they could buy some extra cakes and biscuits for their picnic. Everyone was pleased — especially Sooty. His magic had saved the day after all!